White Lilies Manor

Janina Raven

White Lilies Manor

A Fantasy Thriller

Herstellung und Verlag: BoD – Books on Demand, Norderstedt

ISBN: 9783751977623

A LETTER

Dear Mum and Dad,

It's been almost a year in the Manor for me now, and probably about half a year since we last saw each other? Yeah, on Christmas, I recall.

The situation here is still the same. No change, no development and no news about you-know-what, so I guess that means I'll be spending another year at White Lilies Creek High School?

Normally I wouldn't mind, but lately something about the Manor has been feeling… off. Very much so. I don't know what it is, I can't quite put my finger on it. There's no one I can ask – the two other teens who live here still treat me like I'm not even there. Thought that might be a bit my fault.

Ugh, I'm looking forward to leaving this place behind for the summer and I can't wait to see you guys again! I do hope I don't have to return here ever again.

Don't worry about me, though, I'll survive the coming four weeks somehow, haha.

I hope the cats are doing alright – say hello to them from me, please!

See you soon,
Sparrow

THE BOOK
Sparrow

I trudged up the old stairway of the east wing. Outside, the wind howled and pulled at the roof. Tomorrow there would probably be roof tiles lying on the grass outside the manor.

Lightning flashed across the sky and several light bulbs in the old chandeliers exploded, raining glass shards on the floor in front of me. I sighed and walked on, lighting up the way with my phone's flashlight. The light was only dim, but a year in the manor was long enough for me to remember the way without too much help.

Finally, I stood in front of my room. Whilst I searched for the key in my pocket, my gaze met the book that was lying on the ground.

"Summer Solstice Traditions in England" was the title. Nobody but the nerd Thorne could have left it here for me. He would be the only one to think of giving me such a book. Okay, maybe it even sounded interesting. Worth looking into.

I grabbed the book, unlocked the door and entered my room. Click-clack. No power here either, and though it was only afternoon, it was dark as night. With a sigh, I lit up the candles on the old shelves and flopped down on my bed with my laptop. I put on my headphones and turned up the volume – Symphonic Metal, perfect for calming down after a long day at White Lilies Creek High School.

I took out my school stuff – if I hurried with my homework right now, I'd probably have time to read Thorne's book later.

A Thunderstorm
Thorne

I hope Sparrow has found the book. I hope she will read it. I hope- I sighed and looked out of the window. A storm raged above the vast estate. Not really the perfect weather for my plan.

But wasn't it clear? *Murphy's Law. Anything that can go wrong will go wrong.*

They would get Sparrow first. Then Jasmine. And then me. Sorted by room numbers, like every year.

I had to prevent that.

Jasmine knew it all. She had believed me immediately. She was seventeen. The oldest of us, and maybe also the most mature. She wasn't stupid or quick-tempered. She had listened, asked the right questions and then agreed to my plan.

But Sparrow? She was fifteen, a year younger than me, wild and unpredictable.

As if that wasn't enough, she also considered me an idiot, due to an incident I didn't even want to remember.

That's why I thought it would be a better idea to just leave the book, to make sure she had enough evidence to trust me.

I was no longer sure if I had done the right thing. Would she really be curious enough to read it? *I should go check up on her.*

I grabbed my phone and tried to open the door.

It wouldn't budge.

Somebody must have locked the latch.

WICKED PSYCHOPATHS
Jasmine

So this was how the time here at White Lilies Manor would end for me. A crazy plan, led by a nerd named Thorne and a hatchling called Sparrow – a fifteen-year-old, *mysterious* girl who was distant to everybody and called the whole world stupid. Man, that's funny.

Honestly, I had been glad when I was able to leave the old youth hostel last summer to move here, but now that I knew *why* the rooms here were suddenly free, I wished I was still in that smelly bedroom which I shared with three others. Or even better, in an apartment of my own, in the nearby city. With a job and far away from all these weird guys.

This so-called *host family* was nothing more than a bunch of wicked psychopaths.

Rosary LeDoux was the mother. She and her husband Kyle had a baby, Ethan, who would constantly look at you with his creepy black eyes. Kyle's sister Estelle and their mother Clarisse lived here too, as well as Thill, Rosary's brother. However, Clarisse was doubtlessly the scariest of all creatures in this house. Even more so than the other two teens.

Still, I somehow wasn't able to leave them to fend for themselves. When Thorne had told me everything, for a moment I had thought about simply leaving them. I hadn't had the heart to do so, though.

I sighed and paused the Netflix movie on my tablet – I couldn't concentrate on it anyway. Maybe I should check on the hatchling? I wondered if she had read Thorne's book and if she took things as seriously as you could expect it from a fifteen-year-old. What *could* you expect from a girl her age? Not much, I guessed. One more reason to look after her.

I stood up from my chair and walked over to the door.

It was latched.

Darn.

MURDER
Sparrow

No. Bullshit. That was impossible. Darn. Crap. Fuck. Shit. No. Thorne was just trying to mess with me. And still, this whole situation looked pretty real. Everything made sense now.

The newspaper articles that lay between the pages of the book: *Children disappeared again; nobody remembers them except their parents.*

The explanation from the book's dog-eared pages: *Dark cult on White Lilies Manor kills teens to use their blood for unclear purposes. The dark rite is performed every year on the night of Summer Solstice; with the teens disappearing two nights before the main event.*

While I was still thinking about how damn real that sounded, the realisation came to me that tonight was the second last night before Summer Solstice.

I grabbed my phone and looked for the WhatsApp chat with Thorne. Had we ever texted each other? It was unbelievable how little I knew him and Jasmine despite living together for almost a year. But Thorne was always reading or working on his phone or laptop, just like Jasmine. And I? I wandered around the manor. I knew the whole house by heart, even the forbidden places and rooms I wished I had never visited. The burnt-down North Tower. The torture chamber. That one had been pretty interesting. What had been much worse, was the alchemy pantry. Besides the questionable smells and the typical instruments, I had found animals floating around in preserving jars. The stare of their dead eyes had haunted me in ridiculous nightmares the following nights.

THORNE, I texted, hoping that the terrible cell reception would for once work. WHAT IS THAT BOOK? IS IT ALL TRUE?

I had barely even sent the text off when the door slammed open, colliding harshly with the wall.

"Sparrow, would you please come down for dinner?"

"Estelle?" I turned off the music and quickly shut the book that was still lying on my bed.

"Hey, why so nervous?" Estelle laughed like she always did, but I had seen her frown when she had spotted the title of the book.

"Come on now, we are all waiting for you!"

"Sure." I got up from my bed and shoved my phone and earphones into the pockets of my black denim jacket. *Darn, if this all is true, I'm standing next to a murderer! My murderer!*

Estelle held the door open for me and I lead the way through the corridor. It wasn't a good feeling to turn my back on her, but I didn't want to show her that I knew all about her. No, not *all.* Rather *nothing at all.* I only knew that they were a weird family, and that somebody had put a book with some newspaper articles in front of my door and that – *darn!*

A small nudge in my back had me tripping over my own feet and I tumbled down the stairway. I flailed around, trying to grab on to something until I slammed against the handrails and came to an abrupt stop. My ribs ached from the impact as my brain tried to catch up to what had just happened.

"Oh my, I am truly sorry!" Estelle trotted down the stairs in her long dress and lay a hand on my shoulder. "I did not mean to push thee down there, honestly!"

If I hadn't heard of the rite, I would have believed her. However, I spotted the slight upset look in her eyes and the touch of a sadistic smile on her lips.

"Never mind," I replied, meeting her gaze. "I'm still alive, you know?"

"I can see that." Her face was a firm mask again.

We walked on and this time, I made sure to always stay right beside her.

I had already survived the first murder attempt, and it had been really close. My heart started beating faster even thinking about it, the cold sweat gathering in my palms making my hands clammy. If I hadn't fallen on the handrail, I would have died for sure. A shiver ran down my spine. The steep, long stairway was perfect for murder.

Estelle led me to the hall where the other family members were already waiting. They wore the same noble clothes as always – or how I called them: freaky. Nobody else wore *Victorian clothing* all day long!

Okay, to be honest, it seemed like one hell of a cool way to live. An old manor with a vast estate, and then the residents in their fitting clothes... However, they were no role-play group. They were almost like *real Victorian citizens*, and that wasn't cool anymore.

I sat down in my place. "Where are Thorne and Jasmine?"

"The young lady suffers from a headache, and the young Sir is currently busy with studying." Clarisse cleared her throat.

She was for sure the craziest person in this household, even though they were all weird in their old ways of talking and acting...

"Enjoy thy meal." Rosary smiled a bit. She, Ethan's mother, seemed to be the most normal and harmless person of them all. But maybe I was wrong? Who knew...?

I took the cutlery and looked down at my plate. Salad. I glanced around; the others were eating it too. But who could guarantee that my food wasn't poisoned? I skewered a few leaves onto my fork, feeling pressured by Estelle's watchful eye. I told myself I would just drop it under the table as soon as she looked away, only to realise something was trying to pull me down. In disbelief, I lifted the cutlery higher and higher – and then flung the fork across the table, together with the small, yellow snake wound around it.

Estelle jumped up screaming when the snake flew in her direction, tripping over her long dress and hitting the ground.

Rosary got up to help her, while Clarisse remained on her chair watching my every move.

It was this moment that I decided to run.

Somebody shouted my name. The footsteps following me became louder and louder. *Fuck!* I opened the door to the main wing, rushing across the worn-out red carpet. Darn, why was everything here so complex? And darn! Why was the main door locked?

ESCAPE
Jasmine

Thanks, Thorne. Thanks for nothing. *Go get Sparrow's things.* It had sounded so easy. And now I was hanging above the abyss, on a way too short bedsheet tied to a rope. The chamber of the hatchling was two meters further down, and I was unable to jump or climb up again.

"Thorne!" My helpless cry died away unheard. Thorne must have already left to help the hatchling.

My palms became wet with sweat. I wouldn't be able to hold myself up for much longer. Should I jump? There was a little balcony in front of the window, so with a bit of luck – or rather, a lot of luck – I could make it. Otherwise... I felt dizzy when I looked down.

I let go.

"Ouch!" I landed on my knees, scraping them painfully in the process, but at least I had landed on the balcony. In one fluent motion, I used the crowbar that was tucked into my belt to open the tilted window and climbed inside.

Perfect. Sparrow had a huge backpack next to her desk. I opened her closet and threw stuff into the bag. A few pairs of black jeans, the band shirts she loved so much, a jacket, deodorant. I looked around. *What would I take with me if I was her?*

On the nightstand I found her laptop. *She will kill me if I don't bring it.*

I packed the laptop, and the stuff from its case into the backpack.

What was that on her bed, half hidden under the pillow? A diary.

I moved on to the bookshelf. Besides books, it also held other random items like souvenirs and photos of her family. Half-hidden behind the framed pictures lay her wallet and a pocketknife, which I added to the bag.

That was enough. I didn't have time to rummage through all her drawers.

I carefully opened the door. Nobody was in the corridor, so I sneaked outside.

I wonder if the hatchling is still alive. She must have flipped through the book at least – it was on her bed. Or did the LeDouxes interrupt her, meaning she still has no clue what's going on?

The book! *Thorne will kill me if I return without the book!*

☙ 🕷 ❧

Sparrow

So thou wanted to run away?" Thill and Kyle both folded their arms. Estelle and Clarisse, who stood behind them, stepped aside to let Rosary pass – Rosary, who held her hands behind her back. *What is she hiding?*

"Are we not nice enough for thee anymore?"

"Nice?" My voice trembled. "You want to kill me!"

"Ah, yes. She has read the book." Rosary's otherwise comforting smile became a grimace of horror. She moved her hands from where she held them behind her back to reveal a long carving knife.

My hands became sweaty and I felt around for the doorknob behind me without taking my eyes off the LeDouxes. The door was still locked. Damn, *damn!*

Rosary came closer and lifted the carving knife. A scream of fear escaped me.

"Hey, hey, stop screaming!" Rosary smiled, wild eyes widening with a look of insanity. The tip of the knife moved under my chin and pushed up, urging me to lift my head. I was paralyzed. *Flee! But how?*

"Are you afraid?"

"Hell, *yes, of course! Of course I am afraid*", I shrieked and pressed myself against the door. "What the actual fuck do you expect me to do? Walk around singing and laughing?"

I opened my mouth to continue ranting, only to feel the door disappearing from my back. I fell backwards, hitting the ground. Before I could process what was happening, somebody pulled me up. "Run, Idiot!"

It took me a moment to understand, but my legs were faster than my brain and carried my body clumsily after my saviour. *Thorne.*

"Where to?" I yelled.

"Just run!"

"But~"

"Save your breath, you fool!"

Right into the estate's dark forest it was.

Jasmine

Nobody was around. With the book in Sparrow's backpack, I rushed through the corridors. Someone screamed. The hatchling.

I ran faster, keeping my guard up. It wouldn't be helpful if they caught me too.

Another scream echoed through the manor.

I glanced around the corner to see the front door standing open, with the entire LeDoux family running outside. Even Ethan was there, in Clarisse's arms.

Perfect. For me, at least. Not for Thorne and Sparrow. I guessed they were the reason for everyone storming out of the manor in pursuit.

I flitted over to the forest, into the darkness. Wasn't here... ah, there. The graveyard. I dropped Sparrow's backpack next to Thorne's and mine, which were already lying behind a grave – the name Phoenix Kyril LeDoux carved into the headstone – before rushing on.

I heard footsteps approaching. In one fluent move, I jumped into the bushes and pressed my back against a tree. The wicked chase passed by, leaving me unseen but desperate.

Nerd and Hatchling had no chance; the wild bunch of LeDoux family members had almost caught them. There was just one option left.

"Hey! I'm here! Catch me if you can!" I yelled as loudly as I could, hoping they would hear me – and hoping it would all work out somehow.

🕷

Thorne

In case we don't survive this", Sparrow panted beside me, "thank you!"

"We *will* survive!" I panted. "We *have td*"

"Where's Jasmine?"

"Hey! I'm here! Catch me if you can!"

"There she is." I rolled my eyes. "She's doing something absolutely idiotic. To the right!" I grabbed Sparrow's sleeve and pulled her into the bushes. We fell over each other as I pushed her to the ground and pressed my hand over her mouth.

The footfalls passed by.

I slowly sat up. "Guess we're safe for now."

"Whoa. Whoa, you saved us!" An exhausted smile appeared on Sparrow's face.

"For now", I repeated. "The entire estate is protected by a magic ban on the border walls. I have no idea how to flee from here."

"And what about Jasmine?" Sparrow cracked her finger joints.

"Ew, stop that!" I took a deep breath. "Honestly? I have no idea. This was not planned, you know?"

"And what *was* planned, then? You rescuing me at the last second?"

"Indeed, yes. Maybe not *at the last second,* but rescuing you. Jasmine got your stuff from your room and we have some survival supplies hidden here in the forest."

"So Jasmine knew the entire plan, but I only got the book?" Sparrow hissed. "For what reason, you idiot?"

"I... I thought you wouldn't believe me. I thought you wouldn't listen to me."

"Idiot!" she repeated and looked around the forest. The storm had calmed down and now the silver moonlight played with Sparrow's blonde hair as I could see its image mirrored in her green eyes. She looked beautiful.

Fuck. I should not be thinking that.

"And where will we meet Jasmine if she makes it?"

"I have no idea! As I said, this was not a part of my plan!"

"Ah, the infallible Thorne." Sparrow yawned widely. "We should go to the graveyard. I guess she'll be going there too because it's the only landmark around here. Everything else is just trees!"

That isn't true. What would she say if she knew what else is out there?

Jasmine

Breathing heavily, I sat down on the wall that surrounded the graveyard. I made it. I really made it! They had lost track of me somewhere! Now I had to find the nerd and the hatchling. Maybe they would come here too?

I wandered across the graveyard, looking for the grave of Phoenix Kyril LeDoux. It was a white marble stone, surrounded by swamp green moss.

There it was. Born on December 31st, 1806. Died 2016. He had been old, very old.

"You are such an idiot!"

"I couldn't care less for your opinion!"

"Why, for Heaven's sake, didn't you simply tell me everything?"

"I've already answered that! You wouldn't have believed me!"

"How do you know that?"

I grinned – yes, the others had found me. "A rare live-documentation in fauna! An argument between a bookworm and a hatchling!"

"Hatchling?" The hatchling gave me a weird look.

"You are two years younger than me, what else should I call you? Also, your name is Sparrow! And little birds are called hatchlings!" I replied with a shrug.

"I'm taller than you," the hatchling stated dryly.

Good point. "But younger."

"Could you maybe stop this senseless discussion, Mesdames?" Thorne interfered.

"Mind your own business!" the hatchling and I replied simultaneously. We exchanged a surprised look and high-fived.

"You're so stupid. Typical girls." Thorne rolled his eyes. "Can we now finally go to our lair?"

"Our... lair?" the hatchling asked.

"You have told her *nothing at all*, right?" I mumbled.

"Of course not. When? While happily jogging? Jasmine, we were fleeing from a bunch of killers!" Thorne rolled his eyes again and turned to Sparrow. "We will spend a few days in the forest until we have a plan on how to get away from here."

Sparrow gave him a long look. "Well, that will be fun, won't it?"

SECRETS
Sparrow

I followed the others through the forest. What the actual fuck was going on here? *I'll be spending a few days in the forest. With an idiotic nerd who considers me dense, and a drama queen who thinks she's better than me because she's two years older.* These were the people my life depended on now. Thanks, fate.

Thorne stopped walking. "This place is perfect."

"Perfect for...?" I looked around. By no means could I see a difference between this clearing and any other clearing in the forest.

"For our lair," Thorne replied and dropped his backpack onto the rain-slicked grass. "To be honest, I've planned with better weather, but we don't have a choice, do we?"

"Good to see that you ain't infallible."

"Now please pull yourself together, Sparrow! We aren't alone in this forest!"

"Right," Jasmine mumbled. "Can you guarantee that we are safe here and that our weird pals won't arrive here in a few minutes to stab us?"

"They ran in the other direction." Thorne knelt down to open his backpack. "Also, they hate rain – it will start raining again any moment now. They can't really see in the dark, and they hate the bright light of flashlights. At the earliest, they will appear here tomorrow in the morning. But knowing them, they will probably wait until we can't bear the hunger anymore and will have to get to the house or the main gate."

"But... you have brought food, haven't you?" I asked gingerly.

"Sure." He hesitated, avoiding my look. "But I didn't have a lot of space in my backpack. So I fear it won't last us long."

"Okay." I sighed. "What is the actual reason the LeDouxes are trying to kill us? The book didn't have a lot of information."

"I'll tell you as soon as our lair is prepared." He threw a small package at me that turned out to be a moss green tarp.

⤝ 🕷 ⤞

Thorne

She did a good job, I had to confess. They both did a good job, but Sparrow was a damn skilled climber. She was the one tying the eyelets of the tarp to the trees with ropes, and she looked great while working.

Darn, stop thinking that, Thorne! She ain't stupid. You are, though, according to her.

I looked away from her and over to Jasmine, who was preparing our makeshift kitchen. We didn't dare to make a real campfire, so we had brought a small gas cooker.

The clearing was small and we didn't have a lot of space under the tilted tarp. We had fixed it askew – on one side to high branches, on the other side to the ground – to let the rain water flow off and keep us sheltered from the wind. Our sleeping bags lay in that narrow corner next to our backpacks and the gas cooker on which a tin of ravioli was slowly heating up.

"So." Sparrow sat down opposite of me on her sleeping bag. "Get started."

"With what?"

"Telling me what the actual fuck is happening here, you idiot!"

I hesitated. I had to take care not to tell her too much about myself.

Jasmine threw the book over and joined us.

I took a deep breath. "All right."

Sparrow

Thorne opened the book on the dog-eared page. The newspaper article fluttered out and landed on the damp grass. He picked it up. "You have read it. Each year on the night of Summer Solstice, three teens are killed on the estate of White Lilies Manor. Nobody remembers them except their parents. But why are they killed, you ask? Well..." He paused for the dramatic effect, glancing at me in an oddly mysterious way, but I just rolled my eyes. He sighed and continued, "The whole LeDoux family is... immortal!"

Silence.

Something rustled in the forest.

The rain kept pattering down on the tarp.

"Okay. And...?"

"*Okay, and...?* Is that all you have to say?" Thorne gave me a look of disbelief.

I rolled my eyes again. "Boy! We are attending a school for potentially magically gifted children! About ninety-five percent of my classmates do weird stuff all the time! And you want me to be surprised this family is immortal?"

"Sparrow..." Thorne's voice became serious and faint. "They don't have any magic powers. They become immortal by performing a blood rite, every year during Summer Solstice."

"They- *what?*" My voice broke. "And they use the blood of three teens, right?"

"The blood of three *magically gifted* teens, to be exact."

"Oh. So I guess I'm not in danger anymore, then." It took me a moment to realise that I had said it out loud, and as soon as I did, I wished I hadn't.

"So you.. can't do anything at all?" Jasmine gave me a surprised and almost disgusted look.

"No." I sighed and looked away, up to the night sky. "But I guess as long as the LeDouxes don't know that, they will still hunt me, won't they?"

"Yes. And do you know... *our* magic powers? Mine and Thorne's?"

I looked at her body. "Pretty good hearing, and breaking into houses? And Thorne has night vision, I know that for sure."

Thorne nodded, while Jasmine's eyes widened in unbelief. "How did you know?"

"It was just a wild guess." I grinned. "You wear hearing aids, but they are different from the normal ones. I'm guessing you have them to limit your hearing to make sure all the noise doesn't drive you insane?"

She nodded and seemed speechless.

"You also have a crowbar by your side, and you broke into my room to get my things. Thanks for that, by the way."

"No prob." She hesitated and looked over to Thorne. "Do you really have just one power? Not two? I would have expected you to use your full potential, like the nerd that you are!"

He took a deep breath. "Well, girls, I guess it's time to tell you a secret..."

"Nah." I stood up and walked over to the gas cooker. "I guess that it's time for dinner, before the ravioli gets burned."

⁊ 🕷 ⤳

Thorne

On one hand, I was glad that the topic was changed. On the other hand... I had mentally prepared to tell them everything.

Sparrow put the tin in the wet grass between us and handed us forks.

We ate our ravioli in silence as I planned a thousand ways of explaining everything. That I wasn't a nerd, wasn't a fool. That it was no coincidence that I had found out about the rite.

And then it was time. The tin was empty, the girls had put their forks away and were now looking at me with questions clear in their eyes.

I started explaining.

"Don't you wonder why I know about it all? You know, the book doesn't actually have that much information, but I still know everything. Do you know where I lived before I moved to White Lilies Manor? In the library of the school, because I had no other place to go. I lived in an orphanage before that, even though I'm not actually an orphan. I ran away from home at the age of twelve when my family killed my first real friend. My name isn't Thorne Fox. It's Phoenix Kyril LeDoux."

It had become quiet in the forest.

The rain had lessened and the night had unfolded her dark veil of silence over the estate.

"You didn't run away at the age of twelve," Jasmine eventually replied slowly while watching my every move. "You ran away at the age of 210. You aren't sixteen. You are 214."

"Realistically seen, yeah. But I haven't aged since the first time I joined the rite. For 210 years my body and mind haven't changed. I never questioned it, thinking it was normal. But then I met this boy. He was a guest at our house, just like you this year. He was doomed to death and then my stupid ass befriended him. He was the first one to ever tell me about the world outside White Lilies Manor and the village. When they killed him for the rite, I ran away. It was the first rite in 210 years that I didn't attend. I created a fire in my room in the North tower, faked my death and somehow ended up in the orphanage. Found out my magic power was shapeshifting, so I changed my appearance to prevent being recognised. And when I transferred to the school for potentially magic kids, I immediately applied for a place in their so-called host family to finally put a stop to their games. You know the end of the story. The three of us got accepted and moved here last summer."

"You used us?" Jasmine asked, her voice nothing more than a whisper.

"Obviously." I sighed.

"And you have two magical powers too." Sparrow gave me a grave look. "Both of you do. And I don't have a single one."

"Yes. Yes, you do. At least one!" I replied. I could hardly stand her frustrated look. "Those creeps chose you for the room and the rite! They are never mistaken!"

"Do they even need me if I don't have a power?" Sparrow simply ignored me. "Would they let me go if they knew I don't have one?"

"No. Sparrow, you *do* have a power! You just haven't discovered it yet!"

"Are you sure?" Sparrow narrowed her eyes. "Who guarantees that I can still trust you?"

"You've *never* trusted me. And I didn't expect that to change, even after saving your life!"

She hesitated, playing with a strand of blond hair. "Well."

The awkward silence that followed was unbearable. We lay down to go to sleep without saying another word.

BONDING
Sparrow

I hadn't slept a lot. It was all too hard to believe. In the course of one afternoon, my whole life had changed radically. I was in deadly danger now. Together with a nerd and a drama queen. And the nerd had said that I might have a magic power, after all. A magic power. What I wished for most. My family was highly magically gifted, and though they had said they still loved me without a power of my own, they had sent me to this school so that I got encouraged enough for my power to show up. It hadn't worked yet. And it looked like I was going to die without.

I crawled out of my sleeping bag, stalked over the bodies of the two still sleeping teens and walked a few steps into the forest. I had to pee. It also seemed like a good opportunity to look around a bit.

When I was finished, I strolled through the forest. I completely lost track of time, and walked until I could not even remember where I had come from.

I decided to look around by climbing into a tree, the highest I could find. The higher I climbed, the stronger grew my hope to find out where we were – maybe I could see the border wall and White Lilies Manor from up here?

I couldn't.

But I did see something else.

I almost fell from the tree.

Was I hallucinating? A *squirrel with a unicorn horn?* What the actual fuck?

It cheeped and hopped onto my shoulder. I hesitated, not even daring to move, before carefully touching its fur. "Hey, you."

It cheeped again.

"I'm Sparrow Morrigane, what about you?"

It shook its body, leaving tiny drops of water on my shirt and in my hair. It looked like it was raining.

"I'll call you Rain, okay?"

It smiled – can squirrels smile? – and softly bit my ear.

I laughed. "Hey! Don't do that! Let's go back to the others, they're probably already wondering where I am."

I looked across the forest again. Somewhere between the high trees, the green tarp peaked out.

I climbed down the tree and made my way back to the lair. It seemed longer than my journey to the tree, but I soon recognised some familiar landmarks and before I knew it I arrived at the lair.

Thorne and Jasmine were already awake. More than that. *Wide awake.* And angry as fuck.

"You can't just leave!" Jasmine said. "You must be out of your mind, Sparrow!"

"I had to pee!" I replied. Rain fearfully hid behind my head.

"For two hours? Sure!" Thorne crossed his arms. "You could've at least told us! You know perfectly well that there's barely any cell reception anywhere on the estate, let alone in the forest! You wouldn't even have been able to get our help if something had happened!"

"Just be glad I didn't wake you up! Nothing happened, everything's fine. End of the discussion."

"Never do that again", Jasmine and Thorne replied as one. Right when they had finished speaking, a red bolt of lightning crashed down from the sky, hitting them square in the hearts.

"*What the fuck* was that, my dudes?" Jasmine squeaked, pressing her hands against her chest.

Thorne cleared his throat. "Didn't you pay attention in school? The red lightning marks a magical bond between two human beings."

"So that means we are..." Jasmine hesitated.

"A magical entity." Thorne nodded. The two of them exchanged restrained looks.

I marched across the lair, grabbing my backpack, and waved shortly. "I saw a waterfall over there, I'm going to take a quick cold shower. See ya later, *magic entity.*"

ॐ 🕷 ॐ

Jasmine

She hates us, doesn't she?" I slowly sat down on my sleeping bag.

"Yeah." Thorne nodded and a faint smile appeared on his lips.

"Why?"

"You treat her like a toddler, Jasmine. It doesn't surprise me that she hates you."

"Oh." I slowly nodded. "And why does she hate you?"

He sighed. "That's an unpleasant story. You wanna hear it?"

"Sure."

"Well." He sat down opposite of me, his eyes straying to the horizon. "It was one of the first days in White Lilies Manor. Sparrow and I were walking home from school. The sun was shining, I'll never forget that. It made Sparrow's hair glow."

"I see what's going on here," I interjected but Thorne didn't react.

"I thought, it's now or never, and said, 'Hey, you're really pretty!' She looked at me, took out her earphones and asked, 'What do you see when you look at me?' I said, 'A girl with cool blond, almost white hair and a pretty body, that black clothes suit damn well!' Do you know what she replied?"

I slowly shook my head.

"She asked me why it always had to be about appearances and if I had ever seen her on anything other than a superficial level. Then she told me I'd better start changing my way of thinking or else I'd never find a partner. I stood there gaping like an idiot as she put her earphones back in and walked away."

"Heaven," I said. I was at a loss for words. "Heaven, she might have some brain cells, after all."

"And she knows exactly what she wants," Thorne added.

We were silent again.

❧ 🕷 ❧

Sparrow

After I had taken a shower under the ice-cold waterfall, I put on some fresh clothes and sat down on a rock that bordered the shallow river.

I took out my phone, snapped a few selfies and deleted them immediately. *Stupid idea.* I grinned. *But who cares?*

Maybe I should go back. Back to the others, where I was now even more of a misfit. I didn't have a magic power, they both had two. And now they were a magic entity. *Wonderful.*

The only comfort was that neither of them seemed really happy about it. Yeah, maybe this was what you call malicious joy, and yeah, I felt a little shameful. Not too much, though.

Rain climbed up my sleeve and sat down on my shoulder, softly biting my ear. I pushed myself off the rock and leisurely made my way back to the lair.

❧ 🕷 ❧

Jasmine

What about you?" I finally asked.

"What do you mean?" Thorne pulled his absent-minded gaze from the horizon and turned to me.

"Do *you* know what you want?"

"To get out of here alive."

"That's not what I mean. I mean things... concerning love. Do you have a dream partner?"

He shrugged and his eyes strayed to the horizon again. "Dunno."

"Hm." I hesitated. "Have you ever had a partner? Kissed somebody?"

He kept silent.

I bent over, breathing a kiss on his lips. "Like that?"

"No." He turned around, not absent-minded at all anymore. "Jasmine, whatever you are trying to tell me, I do not love you or anything like that. You are cool, but we're just friends."

"Okay." I tried not to let him see my disappointment and my embarrassment. *How could I even-?*

"You," I continued with faint voice. "You love *her*, don't you?"

"I don't know." Thorne sighed. "And it doesn't matter. I don't stand any chance to be with her. Never stood one. And now we are all going to die here together."

"No, don't say that!" I sighed. *Idiot. If you hadn't kissed him, you could've hugged him now. Just as a friend.*

"Are you finished with your love confessions?" a sassy voice asked and we immediately looked up. The hatchling sat on the branch of a high tree a few meters away, swinging her legs. I had no idea how long she had already been sitting there and what she had heard or seen.

"Sparrow!" Thorne jumped up, bumping his head against the tarp, tripping and knocking over the gas cooker. "Sparrow, it's not what it looks like!"

"I know perfectly well what is happening here." Sparrow jumped to the ground. "You're a cute couple, honestly."

To me, it wasn't clear if she was serious or not.

Either way, this was the moment I made my decision.

❧ 🕷 ☙

Sparrow

Why for Heaven's sake had my heart shattered into a million pieces when Jasmine had kissed Thorne? Why for Heaven's sake did I fucking care about Thorne's choice of girls? Damn! I had been so sure that he had been a foolish nerd! And now I had *feelings* for him?

But even if I did, it didn't matter. He just cared about what I looked like and as long as that was his way of thinking, I didn't even want to talk to him.

"And," I asked with as much happiness as I could muster, "what did you find out about your magic bond?"

They exchanged a look.

"Nothing," Jasmine said.

"I was away for at least an hour, and all you did was making out?"

"Sparrow, please, I-" Thorne gave me a desperate look.

"Yeah?"

"We aren't-"

"I've seen it with my own two eyes. You don't have to deny it." I walked over to Thorne's backpack and rummaged through it, standing back up with a loaf of

❧ 39 ☙

bread and the knife I found in the side pocket. "Anyone else hungry?"

ONE DOWN
Sparrow

A strange sound woke me up in the middle of the night.

I blinked. A silhouette was sitting in our lair, rummaging through our backpacks!

As quietly as possible, I crawled out of my sleeping bag. I felt around on the ground until my fingers hit the hilt of my pocket knife, and I closed my hand around it. Trying not to alarm the intruder, I moved slowly and took on a defensive position when I was within arm's reach. "Hey, what are you doing there?"

"Calm down, hatchling," the person mumbled.

I easily recognized Jasmine's voice. "What are you doing here?"

"What does it look like? Running away!"

"But you can't just–"

"Of course I can, as you see."

"But the ban! And–" I staggered back. "And your magic bond, and…"

"Listen, Sparrow." She placed her hands on my shoulders and gave me a grave look. "I never wanted this bond, okay? Thorne and I don't belong together as a couple, and so the magic doesn't belong either."

"But you…" I hesitated. *Kissed each other.*

"No. *I* kissed *him.* I thought it was supposed to be, with a magical and human bond. But it's not. And I cannot bear it. It just doesn't feel right. I cannot even look into his eyes anymore. I have to go." She let her hands fall to her side. "Maybe, I'll make it through the main gate alone. Goodbye, Sparrow."

She disappeared in the darkness, leaving me behind, bewildered. I should have done something. Stopped her. Asked her if she would send us a message in case she would make it. But I just stood there for a minute before crawling back into my sleeping bag and staring at the green tarp above my head.

Now there were only two kids left.

Thorne and I.

☙ 🕷 ❧

Thorne

You should have stopped her," I mumbled. *Damn. Why hadn't I been awake?*

"But she could be right," Sparrow replied. "Maybe it is easier to flee through the main gate alone. It's better than doing nothing, like we are doing right now."

"We—" She was right. I had promised to have a plan, but we still didn't have one. "Okay." I took a deep breath. "What do you think?"

"Nothing." She shrugged. "It's your plan."

"Damn, Sparrow, you can think for yourself!"

"Are you the two-hundred-year-old son of the LeDoux family who knows the estate and traditions, or is it me?" she hissed. "We need to do something soon because we're running out of food!"

"We do— *what?*" My eyes widened.

"We are running out of food," she repeated. "Jasmine took the rest of the bread, and then there's exactly one tin of ravioli left for lunch."

"Damn. Alright, that means we have only one more chance to escape." I hesitated. "Tonight is Summer Solstice. The LeDouxes will celebrate the occasion with a masquerade ball for immortals. This is the only time the gate is unguarded."

"But we need to sneak into the manor to find out if they caught and killed Jasmine!"

"Yes, I know. And I know how to do that. Or at least, I can get us *out* of the manor because I know a secret tunnel. Getting *into* the house is harder, though, but we will find a way. And concerning Jasmine: they haven't. At least not the latter. Even if they did catch her, they would just imprison her until the rite at midnight. Or torture her, maybe, I'm not sure. Ouch!" I glanced at Sparrow, rubbing my sore cheek. "Why did you hit me?"

"Because you idiot are talking about the life and health of our friend as if you don't care!" she replied furiously.

"Ah, you suddenly have friends now?"

"Damn, *yes,* and they are being just as stupid as I had expected them to be!"

We stared at each other for a few seconds before bursting out in laughter.

Sparrow's green eyes sparkled as she finally said, "So we're going to sneak into the masquerade at White Lilies tonight, right?"

"White Lilies? You gave the house a nickname?"

"Too lazy to say the entire name." She grinned. "I've always wanted to go to a masquerade! Can you dance?"

"No. What about you?" Oh, Heaven, please don't say she wants to dance with me.

"No." She grinned again. "Well, this whole thing is going to end in a catastrophe. Where will we get the masks?"

"You mean, the complete Victorian outfits?" I sighed. "From the dressing room, I guess. But you will hate it."

"I'll simply choose a dress without crinoline and corset. We'll manage somehow."

"I was actually referring to the fact that you shouldn't wear black! It's a mourning colour and it would be really suspicious!"

She smiled. "Sure, if my life depends on it, I'll wear another colour. Except pink. I'd prefer dying."

"Sparrow, we do not have any time to dye your dress!"

"That's not what I- yeah, okay, I know what you mean. I shouldn't say things like that."

"Exactly."

We were silent for a moment.

"I'll go freshen up," I finally said. "Don't make a mess while I'm away."

"Sure."

<u>Sparrow</u>

He had joked. Like a normal guy, not like a nerd. Cute, somehow. *Fuck.*

For a few minutes, I just sat there staring into the void, before I picked up my phone and started filming the lair. In case we made it out of here, it would be nice to keep the video as a memory.

I realised we hadn't even taken a photo with the three of us. If any of us were going to die, the survivors wouldn't even have something to look back at.

I sat down on my sleeping bag, put my earphones in and turned up the music.

Thorne came back incredibly soon. Typical for a boy. His dark hair was still wet; strands of it fell across his brown eyes.

"I realised something," he said.

"Incredible." I took out the earphones. "And?"

"Concerning your magic power."

I sighed. "Thorne, please, I don't want to talk about it."

"No, I mean... you *have* one."

"Thorne!"

"I know what it is!"

"And why would you know it better than me?"

"Because I *saw it!*" Thorne knelt down beside me and placed his hands on my shoulders. "Yesterday, when you sat on that tree stalking Jasmine and me~"

"I didn't stalk you. You just didn't see me," I corrected.

"That is exactly what I am talking about! I looked around and my eyes passed over you without noticing you were there!"

"Because Jasmine distracted you."

"No. Because you have either umbrakinesis or shadow mimicry! Or shadow camouflage, or-"

"Thorne, listen. Please just stop these weird attempts of comforting me. I am mature enough to cope with it on my own, okay?"

"Listen to me, damnit!"

I sighed. "Talk."

"You have to believe me. You can either control shadows or become one. It was the same when I pushed you into that bush when we fled. You were almost invisible!"

"Thorne." I stood up, walking a few steps into the darker part of the forest. "Can you still see me?"

"Yeah. You have to try harder!"

I returned and dropped down back on my sleeping bag. "I didn't try anything in the two situations you named, either!"

"Magical reflexes."

"Oh, Thorne, please..." I hesitated. "Why don't you show me how *your* power works?"

ॐ 🕷 ॐ

Thorne

How am I supposed to show you night vision?" I asked carefully.

"That's not what I mean, and you know it."

"You want to know what I looked like before I ran away? I thought you didn't care for appearances!"

"I do not give a single fuck for if you were hot or not," she replied. "I want to know if you have anything in common with your family. If you look like them. If you smile like they do. If you have the same sadistic spark in your eyes."

"You don't trust me."

"I trust you. You saved me. I just want to know how much you chanced your appearance. If they might have recognised you in the last year. If they know that you are one of them."

"I'm not one of them!" My voice trembled. "Not anymore."

"Not in your way of *thinking*, maybe. But you were born a LeDoux. You *do* have similarities in your appearance! You can't deny it."

"Maybe I had some back then, yeah. If you won't believe in your power, I won't show you my former appearance!" I crossed my arms.

"Okay." She nodded. "How come you have two magic powers and they have none?"

"The rite blocks their powers." I smiled faintly. "That's our one advantage. I have no idea what powers they had once, and I don't even want to know."

"Yeah." Sparrow nodded.

Silence.

She lay down on her sleeping bag, her arms folded behind her head. "Tell me something."

"What?" I gave her a surprised look.

"Well, now that we are... friends, this silence is awkward."

"Oh. ... What do you want to hear?"

"Whatever you want to tell me. I don't give a fuck. I just can't stand the silence. If you don't want to talk, I can also put on my music, of course."

"No, wait, I'll..." I looked around. "Do you want to know why your squirrel has a horn?"

"Mh-mh."

"It was an experiment, about 150 years ago. The LeDouxes wanted to breed new races of fantastic animals—"

"What?" Sparrow sat up. "Darn, they are really one raven short of a murder, ain't they?"

"Yeah. Wait, did you just make up a new saying?"

"I've always used it. But yeah, it's mine. How did you get along with those crazy people for two hundred years?"

"I didn't know anything else, I thought it was normal, you see?"

She nodded and we were silent again.

"Do you know why the manor and the estate are called White Lilies?"

Sparrow hesitated, then looked me right in the eyes. "Because White Lilies symbolise death."

"Exactly." I took a deep breath. "There's a... sacrificial site in this forest. Looks a bit like Stonehenge, just smaller. That's where the rite is performed. Every year after the rite, a white lily is planted there for every sacrificed teen."

Sparrow swallowed and nodded. She was gazing out into the darkness, but I could see in her eyes that her thoughts where elsewhere. "Thorne?"

"Yes?"

"I don't want to die."

"Me neither," I mumbled. A strange emptiness washed over me, leaving me with a hollow feeling inside. As if she was experiencing the same thing, Sparrow scooted a bit closer to me. I hesitated for a moment before laying my arm across her shoulder, relaxing when she did not pull away. Just a moment later, she put her head down on my shoulder, letting out a deep breath.

We sat in a silent embrace.

Sparrow

I had given up.

Given up on trying to hide my feelings.

It just brought senseless inner pressure, and it felt good to just let go.

I had no idea how much time had passed when Thorne finally said, "The sun is almost setting. We should pack the most important things."

"The... *most important* things?"

"Yeah. How do you want to smuggle all of this stuff out of the estate?"

"How do you want to smuggle *anything at all?*"

"We have to get outside the estate, hide our things somewhere and then return to White Lilies to look if Jasmine is there."

"What do you think?" I asked. "Did she make it?"

"I don't know. If only we had cell reception!"

I sighed. He was right. That would've made it all so much easier. Maybe we could even have left White Lilies Manor behind forever if we had known whether Jasmine made it or not.

"Let's go." I stood up.

"What are you doing?"

"Remove the tarp, of course!"

"You don't need to. We will leave it here." Thorne sighed. "I had brought two big bags, but I can't take both with me now. So some things must stay here, such as the tarp. It took up nearly an entire bag!"

I nodded and walked over to my backpack to check if I had anything I could leave behind, when Thorne mumbled something.

"Hm?" I turned around, only to find him wincing in pain on the ground, pale as a sheet.

"You okay?" I walked over to him, unsure what to do. "Are you having cramps? Did you eat anything poisonous? Did you~" I halted in my words when he sat up again. A faint red glow shone through his shirt, but when I blinked, it had disappeared. His voice was hoarse as he said, "Something happened to Jasmine. I can feel it."

THE LAST NIGHT
Sparrow

Once we had packed our things, we started making our way through the forest. It wasn't too long until we passed the familiar graveyard. The full moon that shone in the starlit sky threw abstract, surreal shadows on the ground.

"Full moon?" I mumbled. "Doesn't that mean magic and rites are even more powerful?"

A nervous smile appeared on Thorne's face. "Normally, yeah. But truth is, it's new moon. The LeDouxes always create the illusion of it being full to make it more mystic."

"How? I thought their magic powers were blocked!"

"Right. It's simple alchemy, just like the ban."

"Oh."

We walked on in silence, until Thorne stopped me with his hand and lay a finger on his lips to indicate I should be quiet. I gave him a questioning look until my eyes followed his gaze over to the entrance of White Lilies Manor. The whole family stood there, welcoming their their guests, who wore similar Victorian clothes.

"Perfect." Thorne turned back to me. "As soon as they go inside, we will have to run. Out of the main gate, just run. *Now!*"

I perplexedly rushed behind him. The laptop in my backpack hit my spine and I stumbled, almost fell and staggered past the high brass gate.

Damn. We were outside!

I followed Thorne across the path without looking back.

☙ 🕷 ❧

Thorne

We slowed our pace. Nobody had followed us. They hadn't seen us.

I left the path, dragging Sparrow with me into the forest, which spread outside the estate as much as it did inside. Down below in the distance, flickering lights illuminated the streets of the village – White Lilies Creek. For a moment, I wanted nothing more than to run down there, take the next train and never return. But we had a mission, so I just sighed and turned to Sparrow. "We'll just leave our things here and get them later."

"In case we survive."

"Right."

"Damn." Sparrow put down her backpack and opened it so that her squirrel could hop inside. "We are outside. We are free. And still, we have to go back because *maybe* Jasmine is there."

"Jasmine is there for sure, I can feel it. The bond, you know?" I could still faintly feel the pain in my stomach, as if someone had kicked or hit me. "Do you want to stay here?" I then asked without even thinking about it. "I would totally understand, you know?"

"Why? Because I'm a girl? You sexist idiot." She nudged me. "*You* can stay here if you are afraid!"

"Bullshit. We will do this together." I took a deep breath. "And to be honest, I'm glad I'm not alone."

"You are honest. That's good." She bit her lip.

"You should change into something you won't mind leaving behind at the manor," I proposed because I knew how much she loved her band shirts. "I don't think we will have time to change back into our normal clothes after the masquerade."

"Good idea. Look away." Sparrow grabbed a simple black t-shirt from her backpack and disappeared behind some bushes.

I leant my back against a tree. Things were getting serious.

Sparrow returned, cramming her other shirt into her backpack. "I'm ready. I guess I can keep these shoes on, right?"

She was wearing black lace-up boots, similar to those of the LeDouxes – and I was the one to know it, so I nodded. "Are you ready? Mentally, I mean?"

"Does it look like I'm ready?" She shook her head and a faint smile appeared on her lips. "But I guess I'm doing this for my friend, right? Let's go."

We walked back to the estate in the trees' shadows. At times, our arms touched, but I didn't dare to take her hand.

And then we were back in front of the gate. Nobody was there to be seen.

"Let's keep on walking in the shadows," I mumbled.

"Will we go inside through the main door?" Sparrow asked.

"Definitely not. There's a secret way in through the graveyard." Now I dared taking her hand to drag her deeper into the forest.

"Where is the secret way?" Sparrow asked, then answered the question herself. "Let me guess. Under a tomb slab?"

"Good guess." I knelt down beside a grave and wiggled my fingers underneath the slab.

"Wait, I'll help you." Sparrow knelt down beside me and together we lifted the heavy stone aside to reveal a stairway, leading down into a dark stonewalled tunnel from which a musty smell arose.

"Where does the tunnel end?" Sparrow asked shivering.

"Near the dressing room. To be exact, in the torture chamber. This is your last chance to turn around and leave."

"If only you knew!" She laughed, turned on her phone's flashlight and descended the stone stairway.

"If only I knew… *what?*" I followed her and shut the tomb behind us. The slab closed with a hollow thud.

"Where I have been." Sparrow turned to me. "Did you really think I stayed in my room all throughout this past year? I have been *everywhere* in White Lilies."

"Whoa." I had to smile. "I guess I have to confess that I underestimated you."

"Yeah." She walked on.

"Hey, wait for me!" I followed her. "Do you maybe… want my jacket?"

"Why?" She stopped walking.

"Because you are cold." I gently touched her arm. "You've got goose bumps."

"Oh, it's just..." She hesitated. "Yeah. Please give me your jacket."

I shrugged off my leather jacket and gave it to her.

"Thanks." A faint smile appeared on her face and she put the jacket on before we continued on our way.

A few minutes later, we reached the end of the tunnel. I pointed to the ceiling. "There's the trapdoor to the torture chamber. Are you ready?"

"As I said before: no, but I don't have a choice." She gave me a brief smile. Without any hesitation, she started climbing up the bare brick wall, gripping tightly onto the joints between the rough stones. When she reached the top, she steadied herself before reaching out to crack open the trapdoor. "Nobody's there. Let's go." She opened the trapdoor completely and lifted herself up into the torture chamber.

I followed her – in a less elegant manner – and then we stood there, side by side, right next to several torture devices.

"When I came here for the first time, I thought it was kind of interesting and exciting," Sparrow mumbled. She reached for my hand. "But now that I know that nobody in the LeDoux family would even hesitate before using one of these things, it's just disgusting."

I nodded without looking at her. I had already witnessed how people were tortured here. And I had considered it normal, like the many other psychopathic things that had happened here in the manor.

"Let's go." I dragged Sparrow to the door and glanced outside. The hallway was empty.

"Do we really have to dress up in these Victorian things? They are so impractical for fleeing!" Sparrow complained and pushed me outside.

"Yeah. To get to the dungeons, we have to walk across the ballroom." I opened the door to the dressing room. Long rods with gowns and suits ran across the room.

"Choose something for me," Sparrow prompted.

"Me? Do I look like a couturier?" I shook my head.

"No, idiot." Sparrow grinned, but it was a nervous grin. "But you know best in which dress I will be least suspicious!"

"Oh. Then let's see." I walked along the rows. "No crinoline, no corset…"

"Exactly. I wasn't planning on falling down a stairway because of a weird metal cage, nor did I plan to choke." Sparrow followed me. "What do you think of this one?" I reached for a blood-red dress. "I guess this fits you, even without a corset. You don't need one anyway, it suits your figure." This was the first time ever for one of us to refer to this weird appearance situation, and I had no idea how Sparrow would react. Well, actually, I did have an idea. She slapped me. Softly and with a wide grin, but still: I had been expecting that.

She handed me my leather jacket, turned her back to me and stripped off her t-shirt.

"Hey, where did you get this from?" Without thinking, I traced the long white scar running from her shoulder blade down to her hip.

"Don't touch me," she replied desultorily, but she didn't make any attempt to remove my hand. "It's from a bike accident. Unpleasant acquaintance with some barbed wire."

"Really?"

"Yeah." She slipped on the ankle-length dress. "I'll just keep my jeans on, nobody will even realise."

"Right. Hey, this suits you damn well." I bit my tongue. "I mean ..."

"Yeah." She grinned and turned in front of the mirror in the corner. "Indeed, it looks better than I expected!" She grabbed a huge, matching hat and a black, ornate mask from the shelf and put it on.

"Gloves." I handed her a pair of long black gloves. "I guess a dark colour is fine here."

She put them on and nodded. "I don't even recognise myself anymore, but in a good way. What about you?"

"I recognise you. But also in the good kind of way."

"Man, Thorne!" She chuckled nervously. "I mean: don't you want to get dressed too? We can't stay here forever!

"Oh. Yeah, sure." A blush crept up my face. How embarrassing.

I grabbed a long black coat and a pair of trousers from the rod. "Hey, look somewhere else!"

"You watched me getting dressed, too!" she replied, but she disappeared somewhere between the rods.

I put the coat over the leather jacket – it had been expensive, I wasn't going to leave it here! – and changed my jeans for the cloth pants. Then I forced myself into a pair of narrow shoes and grabbed leather gloves, a black mask and a top hat from the shelf.

"I'm done. You can come back."

She looked at me from in between some dresses. "Hey, Thorne, come over here!"

"Why?" I walked to her.

She hesitated for a moment, then she grabbed me by the collar and dragged me between the dresses and ruffles. "I don't know about you, but I don't want to die without having kissed someone." Her eyes sparkled mischievously. "So how about...?"

I held my breath. "But I thought..."

"You saved my life. I think you are not the worst guy in the world." On her face was a wide grin, but her hands trembled. "And anyways, I don't have a choice, do I?" Her grin faded. "Unless you... don't want to."

"Sure. Never... never wanted anything more." I forced myself to smile confidently.

"Well, then!" There it was again, her mischievous grin. She wrapped her arms around my neck and pulled me closer, our bodies leaning into each other until we were barely a centimeter apart. For a moment, I paused, unsure of what to do. Sparrow's eyes flickered up to meet my gaze one last time as we both seemed to hold our breath before closing the distance between us to make our lips touch.

Hesitant at first, we soon moved in sync, finding comfort in this foreign touch.

I pulled back, having to gasp for a much needed breath and let out a soft chuckle at the absurdity of the situation.

We had kissed. In between all the fabric, tulle, dressed up with masks and hats and gloves. Though I wasn't sure what it meant to Sparrow, to me, it was the best kiss in the world.

❧ 🕷 ☙

Sparrow

I stepped back from him and embarrassedly adjusted my mask.

Thorne stumbled back as well and hesitantly locked eyes with me.

I tried to cover up my insecurity. "Hey, making out with the nerd wasn't even that bad!"

He raised his brows and nudged me. "And what does this mean for us now?"

I hesitated. I had feared this question. Did I even *want* a relationship? With *him*? Damn, yeah. Somehow.

"What do you think?" I asked.

Thorne sighed. "With regards to the high risk of us dying in the next hours, I guess this is the moment to say that I... fell for you."

"Don't expect me to catch you if you are still only thinking I'm hot or something. You waste your so-called love on me, then."

"No, no, I- you are cool. I mean, because- no, you- you are so mysterious, but still- no, that's weird, I just mean…"

I had to laugh. Yeah, he *was* cute trying to confess his love to me.

"Well, in that case…" I hesitated. "You are cool too. And cute."

"For your way of talking, that's an honour." Thorne grinned relieved. "Alright, let's go."

"Yeah." I clenched my fists to subdue their trembling.

We walked to the door and slipped out into the hallway. There was still no one in sight and the silence was alarming. It was clear that we would – sooner or later – meet the LeDouxes and their guests. I just hoped we wouldn't have to dance.

The distant voices grew louder with every step we set towards the ballroom until we finally saw some human beings. They walked through the hallways, happily talking without taking a single look at us.

"Maybe, we will make it to the dungeon without anyone recognising us," Thorne mumbled. "We don't have a plan B."

"We must be truly stupid." I couldn't help but grin. "We are going to die!"

"You should have stayed outside," Thorne said.

"Sexist idiot!"

"No! It's just that they can't really perform the rite if they only have two of us!"

"Why didn't you think of this earlier?" I hissed. "I would've gone alone, then!"

"Shut up." Thorne nudged me. "Keep silent. We have to go into the ballroom now. Try to be inconspicuous, don't walk too fast, don't talk to anyone and just follow me." He linked arms with me and opened the door.

Soft piano music filled the air, mixed in with the near silent rustling of fabric from the dancing crowd. For a few seconds, Thorne and I watched the surreal scene. However, it was not too long before an uneasy feeling washed over me. My gaze strayed across the room, taking in all the people until I locked eyes with Clarisse.

"Rieka, Nero! It's wonderful that ye made it here," she said after a short while of staring. "How about you dance a bit?"

I gave Thorne a despaired look.

"Of course," he said and smiled at me, but his eyes didn't show any joy. He dragged me over to the other dancers. "Just do what they do. Clarisse is watching us, so we *have* to dance!"

Fuck. I tried to copy the moves of the other dancers while Thorne lead me. We slowly moved closer to the door that lead to the dungeons. My face flushed with heat as I tried to keep up with the steps. I knew Thorne was keeping an eye on Clarisse, but I wasn't prepared for him to move as fast as he did. Before I knew it, I was pushed into the dark hallway and the door closed behind us.

"Perfect," he said. "I think nobody was watching us."

"You... you lied to me. You *can* dance!"

"True." A slight grin appeared on his lips. "I just feared you wanted to dance when you asked me, so I lied."

"For Heaven's sake, *nd*" I laughed.

"Okay." His expression turned serious again. "Go down there."

"Why so impolite?"

"Sorry." He rubbed his hands nervously. "I'm just damn frantic. I have the feeling that Clarisse recognised us..."

I hesitated. "Are you sure?"

"No. But eventually, she will realise that we are gone. And she was standing right next to the exit, so she will understand that we went down here. Which is weird, even for normal guests."

"True." We rushed down the steep stairs.

If I hadn't been here before, I would have gotten truly scared by all those narrow cells. But now, I just followed Thorne across the hallway.

I looked through the small metal grid in the first of the wooden doors. The cell was empty and dark: Jasmine wasn't here. I turned to move to the next cell, but Thorne grabbed my wrist. "That's senseless. It'd take us hours like this. We have to take the risk," he told me, took a deep breath and screamed, "Jasmine? Are you there?"

Silence.

"Jasmine?"

"She made it," I whispered.

"But the bond said–" Thorne started, but he interrupted by a faint voice calling from the cell in the back of the dungeons. "Thorne? Sparrow?"

"Jasmine!" I nearly tripped over the hem of my dress as we hurried down the hall that lead to a small cell hidden in a corner.

"I never thought to be that happy to see you, nerd and hatchling!" Jasmine's exhausted face appeared behind the grid.

"Damn, why didn't you break out? That's your power!"

"Not without any tools! Do I look like a magician?"

"I came prepared." Thorne handed her a few pieces of wire through the grid. "But I think we won't need that. Just put your hand on the…

"Thorne, we don't have time for experiments!" I hissed, but he ignored me – and even Miss oh-so-mature Jasmine listened to his every word as he told her to put her hand on the lock. As soon as both their right hands touched the metal, a red lightning shot from the sky. I closed my eyes in surprise, only to open them to Jasmine stumbling outside the open cell.

"Awesome," she said. "And how should I get out of here now? You have your clothes, but what about me?"

I looked at Thorne, but he just smiled. "There's a hidden tunnel in the wall here. Just works in this direction, though, so we had to take the longer detour through the manor."

"Open it!" Jasmine clung to the door. She was white as a ghost and trembled heavily.

"Yeah, yeah." Thorne pressed some stones in the wall.

I felt the tip of a knife in my back.

"Nice dress," Rosary said. "You won't see any blood stains on it."

Jasmine

No! Man, no! Not Sparrow!
We had never liked each other a lot. She was weird and immature. But she had come here to rescue me, and I really appreciated that. She couldn't die.

I quickly glanced at Thorne, who stood there, paralyzed – and still pushing stones behind his back.

"Don't move, or I'll torture the girl," Rosary hissed, a psychopathic smile on her lips. Kyle, Thill and Estelle appeared behind her, long knifes in their hands.

"Thorne," Sparrow whispered faintly. "Jasmine. You have to flee!"

"No!" Thorne replied. "I won't leave you alone!"

"Idiot!"

My God. They are a perfect couple.

Thorne cracked open the hidden door.

I swung around to force my elbow into Rosary's stomach.

Sparrow

I stepped forward and stumbled into Thorne's embrace. Red lights flashed through the dungeons as he screamed her name in pain. "No! Jasmine!"
I turned around. Rosary stood behind us, a bloody knife in her hand. Jasmine lay on the floor, unmoving, in a lake of blood.

"Run!" a scream sounded. It was my voice, but I couldn't remember telling it to scream. Thorne and I rushed through the tunnel, like two remote controlled marionettes.

It sounded like the LeDouxes were right behind us. I ran faster. The tunnel seemed endless...

I glanced back. They were further away than I had expected; the echo must have been confusing me and – *fuck!*

I tripped over my dress and fell to the ground, scraping my palms and tearing the skirt of the dress in the process.

Thorne did not realise I was no longer behind him and I didn't want to call for him either. I pressed my body against the wall. I had only one chance now. *Umbrakinesis. Shadow mimicry. Let's hope Thorne was right.*

I closed my eyes and prayed to merge with the shadows. Imagined how the LeDouxes just ran past me. Just overlooked me.

Just a second later, they rushed past me. Rosary first, Estelle with Ethan not far behind, then Kyle and finally Thill, who was panting for breath. His eyes swept the hall, passing over me and pausing for a second. I froze as a shiver of fear ran up my spine.

But before I knew it the moment was gone and he hasted on, leaving me behind feeling both relieved and bewildered. It had worked, it had really worked.

My entire body trembled and it wasn't long before my knees buckled and I fell to the ground.

Fuck, fuck, fuck.

Jasmine was dead.

Thorne was in danger.

I was alone. And surely not safe yet.

❧ 🕷 ☙

I walked back. Not the way Thorne and the LeDouxes took, but in the opposite direction. The only ones who were upstairs in the manor were Clarisse and the guests, and as long as no one had told them about me, I could stay hidden. Well. As hidden as a girl in a torn Victorian dress with scraped palms could be.

The door to the dungeons was still ajar, but- *fuck*. I had not thought this through. I forced myself to look straight across the room. Not to the floor. Not into the only open cell.

I only realised I had held my breath while walking when I let it go on the stairway. If I was going to survive this, I'd have to look for a good psychologist.

I opened the door to the ballroom. None of the former dancing couples were here anymore. Even better. I crossed the room, opened the door to the hallway – and froze. Clarisse stood in front of me, a rusty two-handed sword in her hands.

I closed my eyes for a second before I leaped forward. I had nothing to lose.

Clarisse dropped the sword in surprise, rising her arms to protect her face as we collided.

We fell over each other. I couldn't tell which body parts were mine or hers. Her bony hand wrapped around my wrist and I let out a scream. I jumped up and broke free from her surprisingly tight grasp. Opening the nearest door with as much force as I could muster, I rushed into the room, hearing the wood slam against the stone wall.

The kitchen. I crossed the room, grabbed a frying pan from the wall holder and stumbled into the next room.

The dining room. A long dinner table was prepared; supper was going to take place here. I scurried on, accidentally catching onto the tablecloth. The dishes crashed on the floor, splinters of china splattered everywhere and crunched under my shoes. Clarisse yelled something.

On, to the next door. *Damn! Stairs!*

The Crow Tower! The higher I got, the louder was the cawing and the clearer became the name.

I had been here before though, and as such I knew that I was lost. On top of the tower was just a platform with a dozen raven nests...

I stopped right on the stairway and held the pan in front of me as a shield.

Clarisse was damn agile for her age and she was right behind me. We crossed blade and pan. Metal hit metal.

Again and again, I had to step back one stair upwards. Until there were no more stairs. I had reached the top of the tower.

The ravens flew away, cawing in anger.

"Thou lost, accept it!" Clarisse swung her sword. "Just like the traitor!"

"The... *traitor?*"

"I am not a foozler. I am talking about *Phoenix Kyril!*"

"Are you talking about *Thorne?*" I turned around and looked down from the tower. *Fuck!*

The LeDouxes brought Thorne to the forest! He was kicking and biting them, trying to escape, but he didn't stand a chance. *Fuck.*

I felt a hand shoving into my back, and then I felt nothing at all.

I fell.

THE RITE
Sparrow

Thorne!" I yelled, and then paused in confusion. I wasn't falling anymore. I was flying.

As if the last days hadn't been wacky enough. Now I was flying above White Lilies Manor, in a Victorian dress and with a frying pan in my hands, sticking out my tongue towards Clarisse and wondering what was coming my way in the future.

From up here, I could see a fiery flickering light from the middle of the forest. The wind carried faint voices to me and I realised that that place was the sacrificial site Thorne had spoked of.

Thorne.

I landed near the fire, somewhere between high trees, and sneaked nearer to the site.

As Thorne had told me, it was a clearing surrounded by thirteen high stone monuments.

Between each of the stones stood a torchbearer. Other attendants carried knifes and daggers, whose threatening blades flared up in the fiery light.

And there he was, tied to one of the stones on the other side of the clearing and surrounded by the armed immortals. *Thorne.*

I crept closer and closer, until I could hear them talking. Thorne was now only a few metres away from me, but still beyond reach.

"We shall wait for Clarisse," Thill said. "She might have caught the girl. We would have two of them, at least. Though it will not be enough for us all."

Good. Then I've got at least some more time.

I gripped the pan tighter and knocked out the nearest torchbearer.

It happened almost without a sound. For a moment, I was afraid of my own cruelty. Then I remembered that they wanted to kill us and that thought even made this kind of enjoyable.

Whack. Whack. Ten of twelve torchbearers lay on the ground, knocked out. I had managed to move around to the other side of the clearing without being seen. They had been too distracted by the LeDouxes' discussion to even realise that all of their colleagues had been taken out.

The other two guards stood by the armed people next to the stone Thorne was tied to, and it was too bright to use my shadow magic there. *What now?*

I hasted back nearer to Thorne's stone to get into his field of reach. Waving frantically from the shadows, I prayed he would be the only one to see me. For a second, his eyes widened, then he lowered his head again. I made a few blatantly obvious movements, trying to tell him that he had to distract the LeDouxes and their guests.

He seemed to understand me, because he changed his appearance to – me? *What the fuck, Thorne.*

I just hoped he knew what he was doing and sneaked closer from behind the stone monument. I picked up a few pebbles from the ground and hurled them across the clearing. The gathered people confusedly turned to where the stones landed in the bushes with a loud crack.

This was my moment. I lifted my dress, got my pocketknife from my jeans and cut Thorne's shackles.

"Quick!" I hissed.

Thorne gave the adults a hasty look before he changed back to his normal appearance and followed me into the forest.

ȧ 🕷 ȣ

Thorne

Sparrow," I wheezed. "What... what happened?"

"Later," she just said and hastened on. Every now and then, she faded into the shadows of the trees, which made it hard for me to follow her. "Your... your power!"

"I know," she hissed. "Now keep silent, Clarisse must be somewhere around here!"

"Ye incompetent foozlers!" Clarisse screamed in this moment. "It is *him! Phoenix!*"

My heart skipped a beat. "How does she know...?"

"I have no idea." Sparrow ran slower.

"Why are you going slower?" I slowed down as well.

"No endurance. Run on, idiot!" Her breath went fast and she was trembling.

"Rubbish!" I grabbed her wrist to stop her and made her climb onto my back. At first, she resisted, but then she gave in and I scurried on. Behind us, flickering torchlight brightened up the forest.

"Roberto shall stop her!" somebody yelled and somewhere far away, a motorcycle engine started.

"Where do you want to go?" Sparrow asked from my back.

"To the village," I wheezed. "Somebody will for sure open their door to us!"

"Let's hope so."

I stumbled through the gate and across the path.

"Let me down. Should we swap?" Sparrow asked.

"Rubbish!"

"Let me down anyway." She jumped off my back and ran on next to me.

The village – White Lilies Creek – wasn't far away anymore, but it was worrying that our hunters fell back voluntarily...

Eventually, we reached the first houses.

"Ring!" Sparrow screamed from a few metres behind me.

I pounded on the doorbell frantically.

"Silence!" Someone screamed.

"Help!" Sparrow yelled. "We need your help, damnit!"

"On Summer Solstice night nobody deserves help!" The man shouted back. "We don't want to deal with your bullshit!"

And it proceeded just like this.

"Aren't you those from White Lilies Manor? Leave immediately!"

"Fuck off, Victorian rabble!"

"It's the clothing!" Sparrow realized in despair. "They think we belong with them!"

I cursed and stripped off the coat, but Sparrow held me back. "Nobody is letting us in! Maybe we need to hide outside, you better keep this."

I sighed and put it on again.

"Where can we go now?" Sparrow asked.

I bit my lip. "Maybe we could break into the grocery store or the cinema and hide there?"

"Bullshit!" She glanced back to the estate on the hill. The light of flickering torches drew nearer. "There are cameras! The only place that we can break into without being seen is... the school, I guess!"

It was silent in the streets of White Lilies Creek. Nothing but the sound of our steps on the rainy pavement could be heard. We left the rows of dark houses behind until we finally arrived in front of the huge school building.

Sparrow peered around. "There in the parking lot is a motorcycle, and look! Light! In the head teacher's office! Someone is here for sure."

I ripped and pushed against the main door. "Locked!" I glanced back. In the distance, torch lights danced on the house walls.

Sparrow hesitated for a moment, then she pressed the doorbell.

"Yes?" The principal's voice didn't even seem surprised.

"We don't have a choice," Sparrow whispered as she clasped my arm.

I took a deep breath and said loud and clearly, "We need your help, Sir!"

Something buzzed and the door opened. We entered the hall.

"Something's wrong here," Sparrow mumbled and turned around, but the door was already locked behind us.

"Let's go into any room," I proposed. "Not to him, but in any random one."

Sparrow took my hand and we ran across the hallways. Stairways up and down. We were alone, and still it felt like someone was behind us all the time. Or some *thing*. Staring eyes. Whispers. A light breeze.

You are going insane, Thorne. And it isn't even surprising after all that you've been through.

"Come over here." Sparrow opened a door and we entered the room.

"Damn, it's scary to be here alone."

"You are not alone." The door closed and a key turned around in the lock from outside the room, then it was silent.

"Did... did you just hear that too?" I whispered. My voice sounded hoarse and I cleared my throat. "Please say you've heard that too."

"Damn, yes." Sparrow nodded slowly. "And it doesn't really bring down my level of concern, to be honest..."

"Wasn't it the head teacher's voice?" I asked.

"The head teacher– Wait, isn't he called Rob by his colleagues? And if it is his motorcycle in front of the school–" Sparrow's voice broke.

"It could have been him that was sent to follow us," I finished, the thoughts in my brain flying around like crazy.

"Do you know what that means? He is one of them, Thorne!"

"Impossible. He ages like a normal person," I replied in a trembling voice. "And he has never attended the rite before!"

"He is their ally! With magic powers! Which explains how he could easily follow us through the hallways... I think he can turn invisible!"

So I am still kind of sane. Good to know.

"What should we do? They will come for us any moment now."

"Now?" Sparrow opened a window. "Now we will flee!"

"Are you stupid?" I dragged her away from the window. "You will break every single bone in your body if you try to climb or even jump out of a fifth floor window!"

"Who says I'll climb or jump?" She smiled and while steps drew nearer in the hallway, she wrapped her arms around my hip and pulled me onto the window sill.

"Are you stupid?" I repeated and tried to break free from her grasp.

"Maybe. But you have to trust me," she replied smiling.

A key turned in the lock.

Sparrow jumped, pulling me down with her.

THE END
Sparrow

Never again. No shit. I didn't think that Thorne is this heavy! We landed softly on the asphalt and I shook my arms.

"What have you done?" Thorne asked and gave me a confused look.

"Didn't I mention? I've got two magic powers!" I grinned at his dumbfounded face. "Clarisse tried pushing me down the Crow Tower, but I can fly, obviously. And now we should hurry to get away from here."

"Good idea. And look, here's our ticket out of here." Thorne bent down to pick something up from the ground. It was silvery and small and–

"A key?"

"Exactly." Thorne took my hand and dragged me over to the head teacher's motorcycle. "Ready?"

I climbed on behind him. *I'm glad I'm still wearing my jeans under this dress.*

"Can you drive this?"

"No, but it can't be that hard, can it?" Thorne started the engine.

"*What did you just say?*"

"Just kidding. I can absolutely drive this. Take care, we are going to get our things now and then take the highway, okay?"

"We... get our things? Back to White Lilies?"

"Sparrow, you might say no today, but you will hate me tomorrow if you don't have your laptop and your band shirts!" Thorne steered the motorcycle on the street and I blushed. He was right.

Two minutes later, I jumped off the seat onto the path and grabbed our backpacks. Rain squeaked and hopped on my shoulder as I climbed back on the seat. Thorne turned the motor around, accelerated, and before we knew it, we were on the highway.

Finally free.

THANKS

Thank you to all my friends on Instagram who helped me develop the plot and characters, gave me advice for the cover designs and for an appropriate price for this book.

A special thanks goes to my friends, beta readers, editors and correctors Mirthe and Inku. You two helped me so much and this book wouldn't be the same without you. (Sounds cliché, but is a fact).

Another Thank You goes to you as the reader. By buying this book, you don't only support me with your money, but you also show me that you are interested in my writing, and that's worth so much more than any money in the world.

THE AUTHOR

The author Janina Raven is a 15-year-old German girl who has already published a novel and novella in German, which are called "Rebel School" and "Tungldraumur".

"White Lilies Manor" is her first published work in English.

She has been writing since her early childhood and besides that, she also likes drawing, photographing and listening to music.

"If you liked this book, why don't you write a nice comment on Amazon or tell me what you think about it via my Instagram account @janina.raven.writing? You can also check out my wattpad @janinaraven!"

Fun Facts

- The plot idea developed from a dream.
- Originally it was supposed to be a German book, but translating it was much more fun.
- It took me only 7 days to write the first draft. We don't talk about editing though.
- It originally had an „I'm not like other girls" character arc for... someone.
- Sparrow's last name was *Morrigan* without *e* at first, but that seemed off somehow, so I added an *e*.
- The idea of Rain developed from a weird photoshop thing I made.
- This book contains twenty-three times the word "fuck" or variations of it and it contains twenty-two times the word "damn" or variations of it. Not to mention all the "darn"s and "shit"s.
- I changed the official publication date... way too often.
- The best part of editing were the comments XD
- The sequels "White Lilies Creek" and "White Lilies Lagoon", that weren't even planned actually, are gonna be released in 2021.
- For more bonus information, such as face claims for the characters, maps of the manor and the area around, or memes, you can visit my Instagram account @janina.raven.writing.